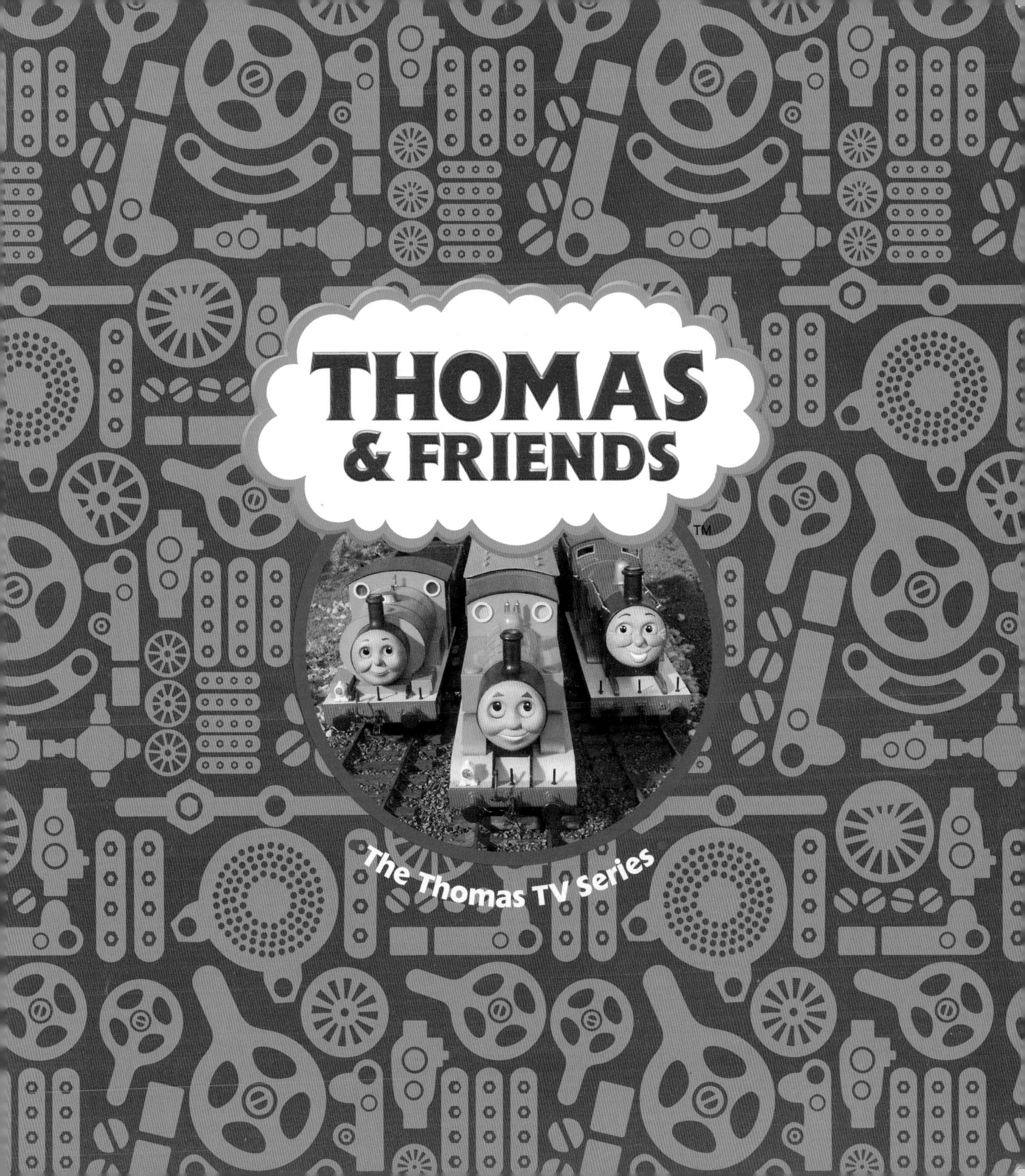
THOMAS
& FRIENDS
TM
The Thomas TV Series

EGMONT

We bring stories to life

This edition first published in Great Britain in 2013
by Dean, an imprint of Egmont UK Limited
The Yellow Building, 1 Nicholas Road,
London W11 4AN

Thomas the Tank Engine & Friends™

CREATED BY BRITT ALLCROFT
Based on the Railway Series by the Reverend W Awdry

HiT entertainment

ISBN 978 0 6035 6684 4
51663/1
Printed in China

RUSTY SAVES THE DAY

Rusty the Diesel Engine worked at the
Quarry on the Island of Sodor.

Rusty's best friends were Rheneas and
Skarloey. Their line ran through forests
and over hills. They loved it very much.
But it was old and messy.

Rusty often left the Quarry to help his friends
keep their line clear. Sometimes he worked
so hard he forgot all about the Quarry!

5
RUSTY

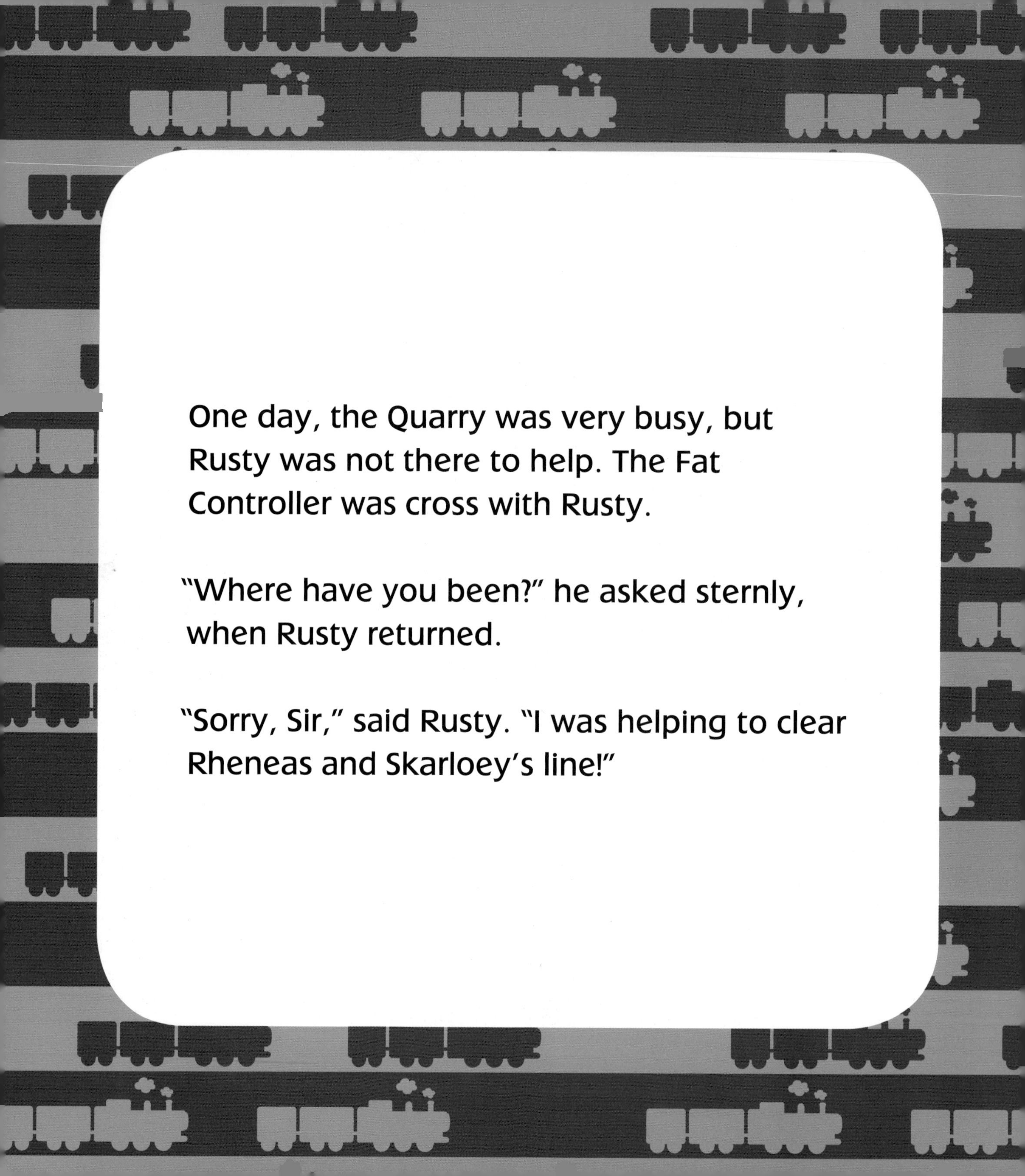

One day, the Quarry was very busy, but Rusty was not there to help. The Fat Controller was cross with Rusty.

"Where have you been?" he asked sternly, when Rusty returned.

"Sorry, Sir," said Rusty. "I was helping to clear Rheneas and Skarloey's line!"

RUSTY

"That line is in very bad condition," said The Fat Controller. "It is not worth repairing it all the time. I am going to shut it down."

Rusty was very upset.

"But what will Rheneas and Skarloey do?" he asked.

"They will come and work in the Quarry with you and Elizabeth," said The Fat Controller.

He had made his mind up, and there was nothing Rusty could do.

The line was closed down, and Rheneas and Skarloey came to work at the Quarry.

They worked very hard, and they tried to be happy.

But they missed the forests and hills. Most of all, they missed their passengers.

Rusty wished that he could do something to help.

RHENEAS

One morning, The Fat Controller came to the Quarry with some important news for the engines.

"We are going to be blasting the Quarry for the next two weeks," he said. "It won't be safe for you here. I will have to find you other work."

USTY

Then Rusty had an idea.

"Please, Sir," Rusty said. "May we spend the time mending Rheneas and Skarloey's line? Then they can go back to their old jobs."

The Fat Controller agreed.

"But you only have two weeks," he said, sternly.

"Thank you, Sir!" said Rusty.

5
RUSTY

There was a lot of work to do. Rheneas and Skarloey's line was covered in rocks and branches.

The track was broken in several places.

The engines worked very hard, but time was running out.

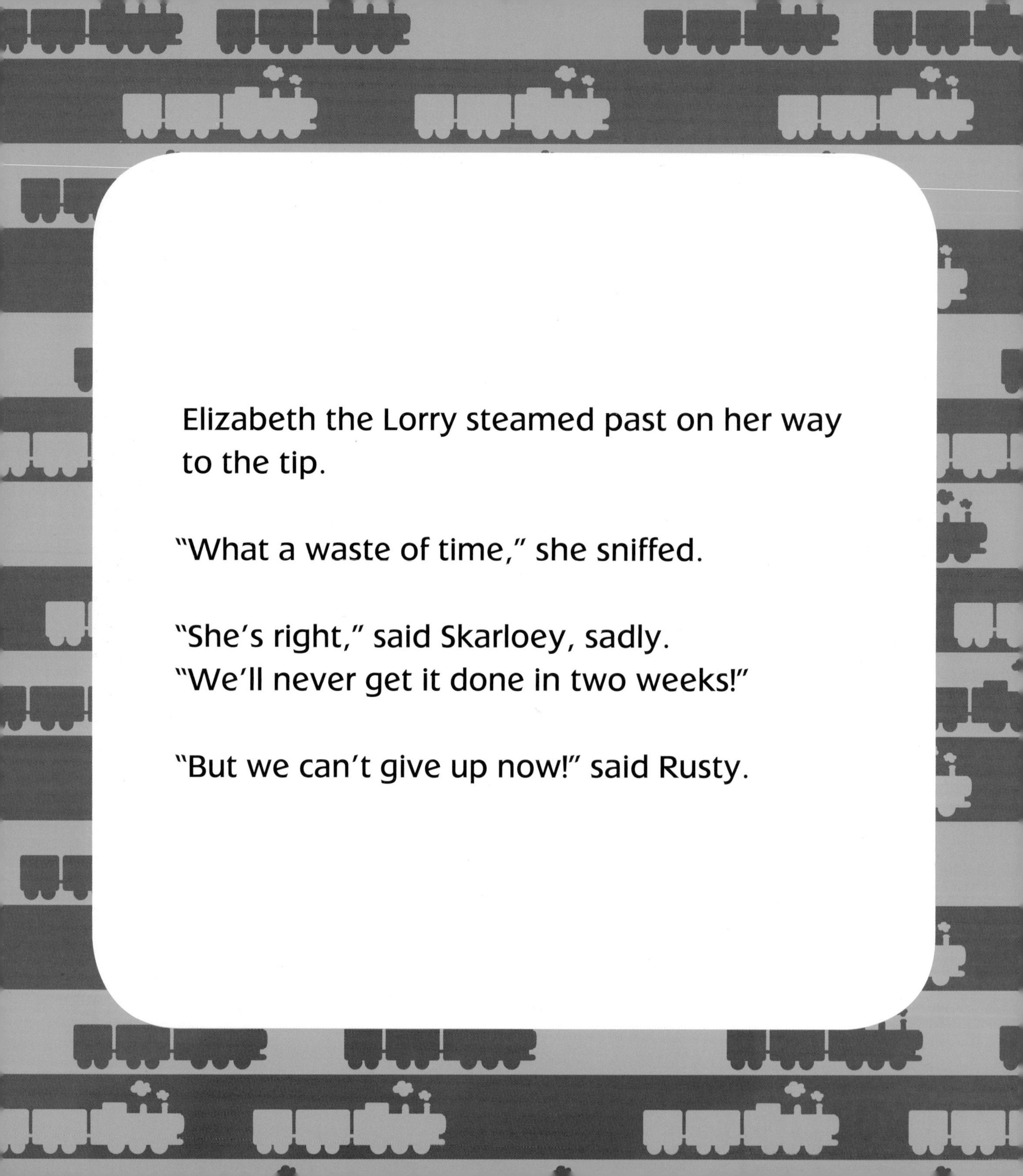

Elizabeth the Lorry steamed past on her way to the tip.

"What a waste of time," she sniffed.

"She's right," said Skarloey, sadly.
"We'll never get it done in two weeks!"

"But we can't give up now!" said Rusty.

RUSTY

RUSTY

Rusty looked at Elizabeth's great big tipper box and had a very clever idea.

"If only we had a lorry to help us," Rusty sighed.

"Well, I couldn't possibly help you. I'm a Quarry lorry," said Elizabeth, importantly.

"It would have to be a very special lorry," Rusty teased.

"I am a special lorry!" huffed Elizabeth.

"You would have to haul!" said Rusty.

"I can haul!" boasted Elizabeth.

"So you'll do it?" asked Rusty.

"Of course!" said Elizabeth.

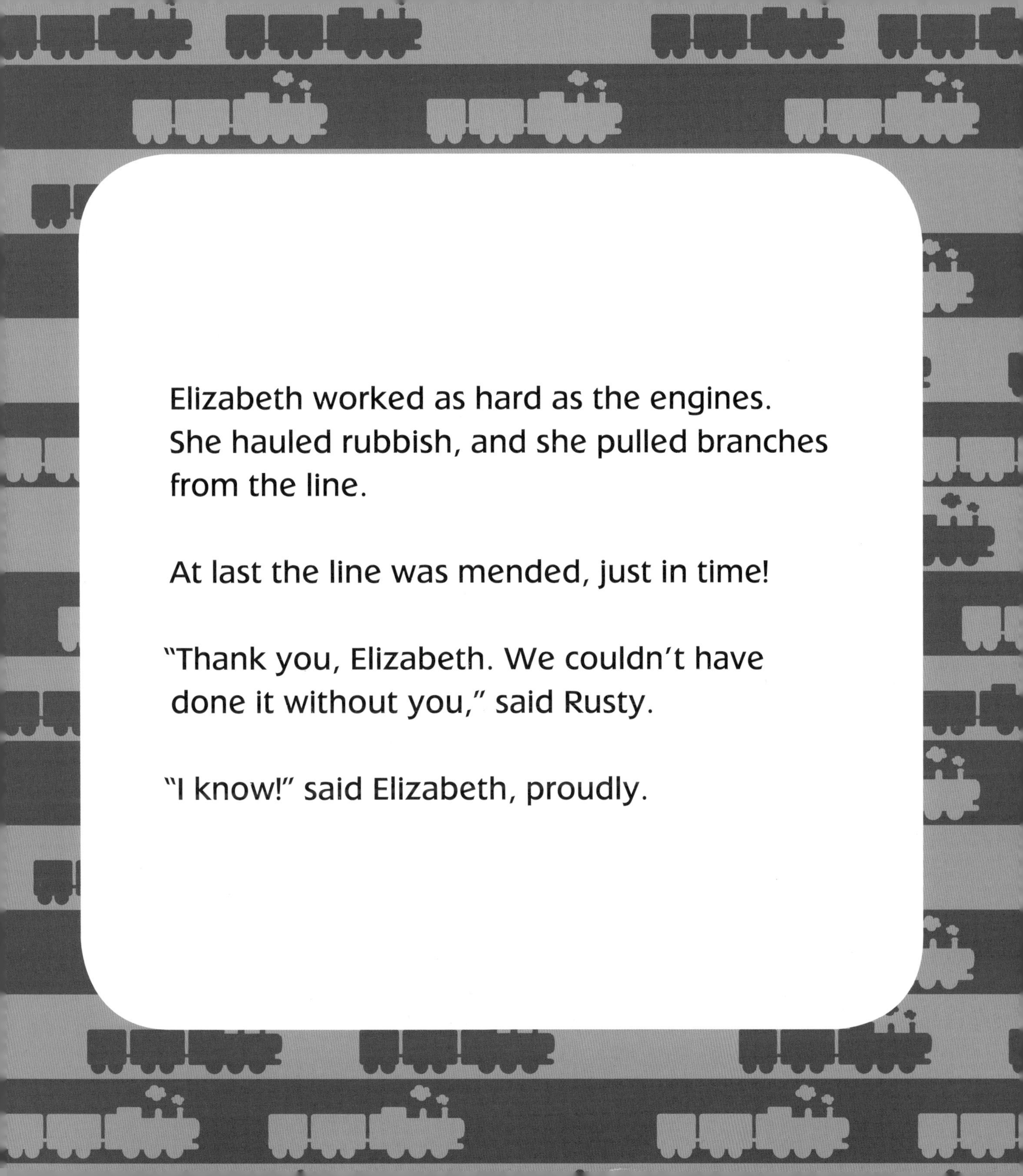

Elizabeth worked as hard as the engines. She hauled rubbish, and she pulled branches from the line.

At last the line was mended, just in time!

"Thank you, Elizabeth. We couldn't have done it without you," said Rusty.

"I know!" said Elizabeth, proudly.

When The Fat Controller inspected the line, he was very pleased.

"We will open this line immediately," he said.

Rusty was proud. Rheneas and Skarloey were very happy.

"I suppose I'll have to help keep the line clear," Elizabeth complained.

But secretly she couldn't wait to come back!